The Almost Adventures of Princess Baby Louie

Written by
Sarah Marie Thompson
& Chris Barker

Illustrated by
Yulia Potts

Nobody knows quite for sure,

but it's said that she was born
a princess of a far-off land.

She loves soft expensive blankets,

and will only eat treats
from your hand.

Her snobbery is apparent,
for anyone can tell,

that she loves to be brushed,
but only brushed well.

Now, this princess of kitties isn't one for the outdoors. She enjoys the safety of windows, fluffy pillows, and clean floors.

You see, her feet are white and her paddies are pink.

She likes to stay inside so
she's close to a drink.

She has two furry roommates
that she really can't stand.

Sir William Wallace and
Little Foosie, who are
both equally grand.

She often thinks that going
outside would be a fun
thing to do,

to walk out the door and
explore the world too.

But in those moments of courage, she has only ever made it out into the garden of plants. She hides behind them, smells them and even eats ants.

But that's the biggest adventure that Princess Baby Louie ever tries. She would rather sleep on her sundeck and rest her golden eyes.

Made in the USA
Columbia, SC
10 November 2017